GIRLS SURVIVE

Girls Survive is published by Stone Arch Books
A Capstone Imprint
1710 Roe Crest Drive
North Mankato, Minnesota 56003
www.capstonepub.com

Text and illustrations © 2020 Stone Arch Books

Library of Congress Cataloging-in-Publication Data
Names: Gilbert, Julie, 1976– author. | Trunfio, Alessia, 1990– illustrator.
Title: Lucy fights the flames : a Triangle Shirtwaist Factory fire survival story / by Julie Gilbert ; illustrated by Alessia Trunfio.
Other titles: Girls survive.
Description: North Mankato, Minnesota : Stone Arch Books, [2020] | Series: Girls survive | Summary: It is 1911, and fourteen-year-old Lucia (Lucy) Morelli dreams of going to college. But for the present, she lives with her large Italian family in a crowded apartment in New York City and works as a sewing machine operator in the Triangle Shirtwaist Factory, bringing home money because her father can no longer work. But this is March 25th, and Lucy will soon be fighting for her life as fire sweeps through the locked-down factory, trapping the workers inside.
Identifiers: LCCN 2019003165 | ISBN 9781496583864 (hardcover) | ISBN 9781496584489 (pbk.) | ISBN 9781496583918 (ebook pdf)
Subjects: LCSH: Triangle Shirtwaist Company—Fire, 1911—Juvenile fiction. | Fires—New York (State)—New York—History—Juvenile fiction. | Clothing factories—New York (State)—New York—Juvenile fiction. | Italian American girls—Juvenile fiction. | Immigrants—New York (State)—New York—Juvenile fiction. | Survival—Juvenile fiction. | New York (N.Y.)—History—1898–1951—Juvenile fiction. | CYAC: Triangle Shirtwaist Company—Fire, 1911—Fiction. | Italian Americans—Fiction. | Immigrants—Fiction. | Survival—Fiction. | New York (N.Y.)—History—1898–1951—Fiction. | LCGFT: Historical fiction.
Classification: LCC PZ7.1.G549 Lu 2020 | DDC 813.6 [Fic]—dc23
LC record available at https://lccn.loc.gov/2019003165

Designer:
Charmaine Whitman

Image credits:
Library of Congress, 106; Newscom: Everett Collection, 108;
Sarah Byrnes, 112; Shutterstock: kaokiemonkey (pattern), back cover and throughout, Max Lashcheuski (background), 2 and throughout

Printed and bound in the USA.
PA70

LUCY
FIGHTS THE FLAMES
A Triangle Shirtwaist Factory Survival Story

by Julie Gilbert

illustrated by Alessia Trunfio

CHAPTER ONE

Greenwich Village, New York City
Morelli family's tenement
March 25, 1911
7:00 a.m.

I woke to the sound of an argument. Angry voices muttered in Italian and disturbed the quiet morning.

I groaned, rolling onto my side. I tried to slide back into the wonderful dream I'd been having. I'd been wearing a flowing gown and dancing among the stars. Halley's Comet had shot past, and I'd grabbed a handful of its tail. Then I'd entered a magical laboratory and discovered that the tail was made of diamonds and fairies.

I wrinkled my nose as the dream faded. Everyone knew the comet's tail was composed of dust particles and gas. When it had passed by Earth last year, some newspaper had claimed that the comet's tail was poisonous.

People had panicked, believing Earth would be destroyed. But not me. The moment I saw the bright streak in the sky, I fell in love. I wanted to learn everything I could about the universe. It was the moment I knew I wanted to be an astronomer.

Across the room, the argument grew louder. My father and sixteen-year-old brother, Tony, tried to keep their voices low, but in a cramped tenement, there was no privacy. I could hear the word *union* clearly, followed by angry whispers.

I sighed and stretched. My neck was stiff. That happened a lot when you slept on the kitchen table all night. I'd have preferred a fluffy feather bed, but the only bed we had was shared by our two renters in the tiny bedroom. Even my parents didn't sleep in a bed.

A tiny finger poked me between my shoulder blades. I turned and saw the dark eyes of my ten-year-old sister, Alessandra, staring at me.

"What's a union?" Alessandra whispered.

I sighed again. Clearly I wasn't the only one who'd overheard. "It's when a group of workers band together," I explained. "They elect leaders and try to negotiate with their employers."

Alessandra looked confused. "Why?"

"To fight for workers' rights. Unions want better working conditions, like shorter hours and better pay. Sometimes they go on strike if their employers don't listen. Do you know what a strike is?"

"It's when people stop working," Alessandra replied.

I nodded. "Right. And if there are no workers, the employers don't make money."

Alessandra processed this for a few moments. Now that I was fourteen, unions and factory work were a way of life for me, but it was probably a lot for a ten-year-old to take in.

Across the room, my father paced back and forth across the thin carpet. On the sofa, two more of my siblings stirred. The chair where my mother usually slept was empty. She was probably at the market buying milk.

"You know what happens to people in unions!" Papa shouted, no longer trying to keep his voice low.

Alessandra looked nervous. "What happens to people in unions?" she whispered. "Why is Papa so mad at Tony?"

"If his bosses at the docks knew Tony was involved with the unions, they could fire him," I explained. "Employers don't like unions."

"What would we do if Tony got fired?" Alessandra worried.

I pressed my lips together. "We'd figure it out. I'd still have my job."

But privately I shared my sister's worries. Ever since Papa's accident last summer, we'd been living on the edge of poverty. I made roughly six dollars a week at the Triangle Shirtwaist Factory. Tony made a little more at the docks. Our mother took in laundry, and we had rent from our two boarders. But even then, we barely had enough to buy food. We paid twelve dollars a month in rent, and the landlord was threatening to raise the rate if Mama had another baby.

"Come on," I said, trying to distract my sister. "Let's get the table straightened before Mama comes back."

Alessandra jumped to her feet and folded our thin blankets. I quickly braided her dark hair and then brushed my own, tying it back with a faded ribbon. Around us, the tenement came to life.

As the oldest girl, I was in charge of the house until Mama came back. I made sure everyone folded their sheets and got dressed. I changed the baby and swept the floor. I stirred the oatmeal that Mama had started before dawn. I scrubbed down the counter, trying to make a dent in the grime that covered every surface. Thanks to the coal stove that belched dark smoke, it was a losing battle.

The entire time, Tony and Papa argued. Finally, I'd had enough. I strode up to them and propped my hands on my hips. "Can you please stop?" I demanded.

Papa frowned, clutching his mangled arm closer to his chest. He did not like it when I spoke up.

"Lucia, this is not for you," Papa barked.

"Mama will be home soon. She's not going to want to hear you arguing," I said.

"What she will not want to hear is that your brother is involved with the unions!" Papa bellowed.

"She already knows," Tony interrupted.

Papa looked shocked.

"Papa, all we are trying to do is make the factory owners listen," Tony continued. "Take the International Ladies' Garment Workers' Union." Tony had started volunteering with them after I got my job at Triangle. "They're pushing for better pay, especially at Triangle. Shorter work hours. Safer conditions."

"Waste of time," Papa scoffed. "They will never listen to you."

"It's worked before," Tony insisted. "Don't you remember the strike two years ago? All those women walking off the job, organizing and standing up to the factory owners? There were twenty thousand of them! They succeeded. They got shorter hours and better pay for girls just like Lucy."

"Not at Triangle," Papa said.

"No, not there," Tony conceded. "But that doesn't mean the work is not worth doing. If enough of us raise our voices, the factory owners will be forced to listen."

Papa shook his head. "Men like that don't listen. They will find other immigrants who will work in those same factories for the same pay—maybe less. Better to keep your head down and keep your job."

"It's worth a try," Tony said. He ran a hand through his dark curls in frustration. "You want Lucy to have safer working conditions, don't you? Or do you want her to get hurt too?"

I froze. We never mentioned Papa's arm. He had injured it unloading crates down on the docks. The crane had snapped, and a crate fell on Papa, crushing his arm.

Papa glared at Tony and waved him away with his good hand. "What happened to me was an unfortunate accident. I do not blame my boss for firing me. My arm was hurt. I was no longer a good worker. Why would they keep me?"

"Papa—" Tony started.

"No. I will not hear it." Papa stuck his finger in Tony's face. "You keep your head down and do your work. Do you hear me?"

I opened my mouth to protest, but Papa turned on me. "No, Lucia. This is not for you. You go to your job and you earn your keep."

I held his gaze for a long, terrible moment. Then I said, "I go by Lucy now. Not Lucia."

Papa stared at me. I knew using the Americanized version of my name upset him, but I was taking a stand. I was not his obedient Italian daughter. I was my own person, with my own hopes and dreams. The truth is, I had never been very obedient. I had just been good at keeping it a secret.

Before he could respond, the door to the apartment creaked open, and Mama came inside. She wore a threadbare coat and a battered hat. A basket was draped over her arm.

"What is it?" she asked, her voice tight as her eyes roved over the apartment.

"Tony and Papa were fighting again," Alessandra volunteered.

I was too far away to kick her shin to keep her quiet. Mama hated when Tony and Papa fought. I settled for sending my sister a dirty look. Alessandra stuck her tongue out at me.

"Lucia. Come help me with breakfast," Mama said after shooting a warning frown at Papa. "And I don't want to hear any more arguing this morning."

"You knew what Tony was doing? With the unions?" Papa demanded.

Mama glared at him. "As long as he stays safe, it is not my business."

Papa harrumphed and plopped down on the couch to wait for his food. I followed Mama to the kitchen.

"Never enough space and always too much fighting," Mama muttered under her breath as she grabbed the frying pan.

She's right, I thought, looking around our tenement. It had a grand total of three rooms: a kitchen, a parlor, and the bedroom. Since we rented out the bedroom for extra income, the eight members of my family were crammed into the kitchen and parlor.

When Papa first brought us here from Italy ten years ago, this was supposed to be a temporary stop. Papa had dreamed of a prosperous farm in the country, of rich soil and plenty of rainfall, unlike the farm we had left behind in Italy. But land in America was expensive, and soon there had been more and more mouths to feed. We could never save enough. Now we were just trying to survive.

"Lucia, the oatmeal," Mama said, interrupting my thoughts.

I moved the pan, wrinkling my nose at the smell.
The entire tenement would smell like scorched
porridge for the next few days. At least it would help
cover the smell of trash that wafted up the air shaft.

"Mama, he can't keep me from the unions," Tony
said, appearing in the doorway. He kept his voice low,
although I'm sure Papa could hear every word.

"I'll talk to him later," Mama said.

"It's not fair!" I blurted, the words bursting from my mouth. Everyone stopped and stared at me. My mother, Tony, my younger siblings. Papa scowled at me from the sofa. Even the baby looked up from where he was chewing on a clean rag.

I had their attention now.

"It's not fair!" I repeated. "Why is Tony allowed to be involved with the unions, and I don't get to do what I want to do?"

Mama looked at me with raised eyebrows. "And what is it that you want to do, Lucia?"

I drew a deep breath. "I want to go to school." I had never spoken those words aloud to my family before.

"What school?" Papa demanded.

"I can take classes at the Cooper Union," I said. "Evening classes, but if I work hard enough, I could go to college there when I'm older. Study science." Once the words were out, I couldn't take them back.

Papa rose to his feet. "No," he said.

"No?" I repeated. "That's it?"

"You do not need school," Papa said firmly. "You will make money for the family, and when you're old enough, you will marry a nice boy and settle down."

"But Papa—"

He cut me off. "If you have enough time for evening classes, you have enough time for work. Take in extra mending or laundry. You have no need for an education."

My eyes filled with tears, and I turned to Mama. Surely she would understand. "Please."

Mama looked at me with a thousand heartaches in her eyes. "Lucia," she murmured. "Your father is right. I'm sorry."

I slammed my hands on the counter. "It's not fair!"

The noise startled the baby. His eyes filled with tears, his face wrinkled, and then he started bawling.

"Now look what you've done," Mama scolded me. She wiped her hands on her apron as she went to comfort the baby.

I stood in the kitchen, my fists clenched against overwhelming anger and frustration. Alessandra looked angry, and Tony looked grim. The baby kept crying. Papa turned his back on me.

A sob rose in my throat, and without another word, I grabbed my coat and hat. I had to get to work. As I ran out of the tenement, the weight of my future pressed against my chest. The factory was waiting for me. It was the only future I was allowed to have.

CHAPTER TWO

I stormed down four flights of stairs, bumping my shoulder on the doorframe as I spilled onto the sidewalk. A few of my neighbors waved, but I ignored them. I was already late getting to work.

I had been a sewing machine operator at the Triangle Shirtwaist Factory for the past few months, ever since it had become clear that Papa couldn't return to work. I sewed shirtwaists for women. Well, I really only sewed sleeve pieces together. Hundreds and hundreds of sleeves each day. I sat in a long row with other girls who also sewed sleeves. If I was lucky, they might let me sew collars in a few years.

A sewing machine operator, I thought. *That is my future. Not astronomy.* I gritted my teeth to keep the tears in my eyes from spilling down my face.

Halfway down the block, Tony caught up with me. "Lucy, wait," he said, tugging on my elbow.

"What?" I demanded as I whirled on him.

My brother held up my lunch pail. The metal handle dangled from his fingers. "Thought you might want this."

I snatched the pail from him. "Fine. Now go away!"

Tony held up his hands in a gesture of peace. "I'm only trying to help."

"I know," I relented. I let the pail drop to my side and gave him an apologetic smile.

"We picking up Cara?" Tony asked, falling into step beside me. Lately he had fallen into the habit of walking me to work before heading to his job at the docks.

I nodded. Our cousin Cara worked at Triangle, just like I did. In fact, she'd gotten me the job. Cara was almost twenty and already engaged to a man named Frank. He worked as a cutter, which was one of the most prestigious jobs at the factory. It took skill and strength to cut through layers of fabric to make shirtwaist pieces.

Tony and I walked without speaking for a few blocks. The silence between us didn't bother me. My brother and I were used to giving each other space to think. Living with ten people in a tiny apartment taught you to respect each other's privacy.

Besides, it was hard to have a conversation on Bleecker Street. Merchants shouted from their stalls, advertising the low price of their meat or the freshness of their greens. Young men flirted with some of the factory girls near the bowling alley. On the corner, a mother scolded her sobbing child while a horse-drawn wagon clattered over the cobbled street. The scent of bread from the nearby bakery filled the air and made my stomach rumble. I hadn't eaten breakfast before I stormed out of the tenement.

"I want you to go to school," Tony said as we turned a corner down a quieter side street. "No matter what Papa thinks. It's why I'm helping the unions. I want you to have better opportunities. I want *all* of us to have better opportunities."

"Papa wouldn't allow it, even if I could work fewer hours for better pay," I said, my voice flat. "You heard him."

"Don't let him stop you," Tony said. "I haven't."

I couldn't think about Papa. Deep down I knew he had a point. Even if I had time for classes, that time would be better spent earning more money for the family.

"You really think the unions can make some changes at Triangle?" I asked, changing the subject.

The unions made me nervous. I remembered the strikes a few years ago. Crowds of women and men had walked the picket line, demanding better working conditions. Then came the strikebreakers. The factory owners had hired them to beat up the strikers, hoping that the workers would be scared enough to go back to work. Tony had ended up with a black eye and two cracked ribs. I didn't want to see him get hurt again.

"Triangle isn't that bad," I finally said.

Tony made a scoffing noise.

"No, I mean it," I said. "I don't like the noise or how cramped it is. Or how they lock us in so we can't leave early. Or how they sometimes change the clocks so we have shorter lunch breaks. And I really hate that they dock our pay when we make a mistake."

"But other than that, it's great," Tony joked grimly.

"Well, maybe it isn't so great," I admitted. "But it is a job. A job that puts food on our table and clothes on our backs. Maybe keeping your head down and getting paid isn't so bad."

"You sound just like Papa," Tony said.

I shoved his shoulder—hard. "No, I'm not! You take that back!"

Tony shook his head and rubbed his arm. "You and he have the same temper. It makes sense you'd share the same views about unions."

"Not unions," I said. "Work—and the necessity of it." I whirled around to face my brother, emotion welling up within me. "How else will we eat?" My voice broke. I shifted my lunch pail and tugged at my scarf. I was trying not to cry. "Let's go get Cara."

We walked in silence for another half block, then came to a stop in front of the three-story tenement where Cara lived. I was surprised she wasn't already outside waiting for us, like usual. I knocked on the door, its exterior grimy with soot.

A few minutes later, the door opened slowly, and Cara peered out. Her eyes were puffy and her nose was red.

"I can't go to work today," she said, coughing into a handkerchief. "I'm too sick."

"You sure?" I asked. "You're going to lose a day's worth of pay. They might demote you. You'd be stuck sewing basic seams with me instead of fitting bodices."

"Maybe I'd be able to sit next to you at least," Cara said with a tired smile. "I'm sure, though. I'm achy all over, and the room spins when I walk. Frank and I have a date tomorrow, and I want to be better by then."

"But it's payday," I pointed out.

"I'll have to wait until Monday, I guess," Cara said. "I feel awful."

She looked awful too. There was no arguing with that. "I'll see if I can get your pay," I offered.

"Do you want Rosie and me to bring you some soup later?"

Since it was Saturday, we only had to work until four thirty. I was already excited to spend the evening with my best friend.

"Thank you," Cara said, her face brightening a little. "I would like that. Oh, can you bring this note to Frank?" She shoved a piece of paper into my hand.

"Um, sure." I pocketed the note.

Cara sneezed as she closed the door. Both Tony and I jumped back to avoid the spray.

"C'mon, you don't want to be late," Tony said as we walked into Washington Square Park.

A cold wind blew through the park, making the trees shiver. I pulled my thin coat closer around me. I was looking forward to milder temperatures, at least before the heat of summer hit and the neighborhood started to reek of hot garbage.

"You don't have to walk me every day," I said. "This is already the third time this week."

Was it my imagination, or did Tony stumble slightly?

"It's nice to get out of the apartment," he said, clearing his throat. "At least for a little bit."

"You have work today, don't you?" I asked.

Tony nodded. "Well, sure."

"And work is in the opposite direction," I said.

"As I said, it's nice to stretch my legs," Tony stated.

His tone made it clear he was not interested in continuing the discussion. I wasn't ready to let it drop, however. I suspected the real reason he was walking with me had nothing to do with stretching his legs.

"You're not hoping to run into anyone, are you? Say, a certain Rosie Birnam?" I prompted. Rosie was my best friend and we worked at the factory together. Tony met her a few months ago. His face lit up whenever I mentioned her name.

"Quiet, you," Tony said, but he was blushing.

By that time, we had arrived at the Asch Building. It looked like most other factories, all tall windows and a dingy gray facade. Triangle occupied the eighth, ninth, and tenth floors of the building.

I joined the line of workers waiting for the freight elevators near Greene Street. We weren't allowed to use the passenger elevators on Washington Place. Only management and paying customers could use the passenger elevators—company policy.

"Well," Tony said, shoving his hands into his back pockets. I could tell he was trying to stall.

I opened my mouth to tease him some more when someone shrieked, "Rat! A rat!"

The line of workers surged and parted, followed by more screams and shouts. I saw the sleek body of the rat weaving through the crowd just as someone elbowed me in the back. I almost kept my feet beneath me, but the crowd surged again.

Tony's face grew alarmed as we got separated. He reached for me, but it was too late.

I fell to the ground.

CHAPTER **THREE**

Triangle Shirtwaist Factory
March 25, 1911
8:30 a.m.

"Lucy! Lucy, are you OK?"

I recognized my best friend's voice. A moment later, I spotted Rosie pushing through the crowd to get to me. It was no easy task, given her size. I was small for my age, but Rosie was even smaller. She had dark hair and brilliant, flashing eyes that were usually filled with laughter.

"Give her some space!" Rosie yelled when she finally made her way to me. "Lucy! Are you OK?" She dropped to the sidewalk.

"I'll be fine," I said. "I think I tore my hem, though."

"Hmm . . . now where would we ever find a needle and thread to fix it?" Rosie asked, a smile dancing around her mouth.

"I know a place . . . if you aren't worried about getting fired," I said.

The foremen at Triangle searched our bags and pockets each night to make sure we hadn't stolen even a scrap of lace. They'd fire me in an instant if I used a machine to fix my dress.

"We'd run away," Rosie said. "Join a traveling stage show and become actresses. Or find a circus! I'd fly high on the trapeze, and you'd walk the tightrope. We'd break hearts in every town we visited."

"Are you finished?" Tony asked, standing over us. He was smiling broadly. Rosie grinned up at him and wrinkled her nose.

"You didn't let me get to the best part! Two mysterious princes fall in love with us and send us to college. It will be quite romantic," Rosie confided to me.

"Also practical," I said.

"Come on, you two," Tony said, bending down to give each of us his hand.

I watched Rosie's normally steady hand tremble a little in Tony's grip. "Thank you, Sir Antonio," she said when we were on our feet.

"At your service, madam," Tony replied, giving us both an elegant bow. His gaze lingered a moment on Rosie. "I'd better get to work."

As Tony walked in the direction of the docks, I gave Rosie a questioning look.

"What?" she asked.

"Nothing. Except this is the third time Tony's walked me to work in a week. And I think we both know why," I said.

Rosie's face turned solemn. "Nothing will ever happen between me and your brother. As much as I'd love to be your sister," she added.

"You already are," I said. We edged forward in line to the elevator.

Rosie squeezed my hand. "It's not so simple. First of all, I'm way too young to get married. And I want to go to college." She pressed her lips together. "And I'm a Russian Jew. Tony is an Italian Catholic. Neither of our families would ever approve."

Rosie was right, I knew. There was no getting past those barriers. I hadn't even mentioned Rosie to my parents. I didn't know how they would react. Even though we lived in America, they expected me to be Italian. I was supposed to spend time with other Italian girls and meet a nice Italian boy and make little Italian babies. Tony was supposed to find a nice Italian girl as a bride.

"Let's stick with our plan," Rosie said. "Save money. Go to college. Just like we've dreamed."

"I . . . I hope we can still do that," I said.

Rosie searched my face. "What happened?"

I shrugged. "I told Papa that I wanted to take evening classes at the Cooper Union. He said no."

My voice broke, and Rosie gave me a quick hug as we made our way into the factory building. As we stepped onto the elevator, she drew me into the corner. "We'll fix this," she said. "I don't know how, but we will. It's a challenge. And try to remember, there are far worse problems in the world."

Rosie and I never talked much about our lives before coming to America—"Better to focus on the future," she would say whenever I asked—but I knew she and her family had witnessed horrible persecutions and pogroms before coming to America.

Once, after I pressed her, Rosie had told me in flat tones how all the Jewish businesses in her town had been looted and burned as the authorities watched. Her family's home had been destroyed, and they'd fled, fearing for their lives.

I nodded, sniffling as the elevator carried us skyward. I knew Rosie was right. There were far worse problems in the world. But the idea of me going to college and becoming an astronomer seemed so far away, especially after this morning's fight with Papa.

"Listen, I can't get down for lunch today, but I'll see you after work, OK? We'll get food at one of the food carts and catch a lecture in the Great Hall," Rosie said as the elevator doors opened onto the eighth floor.

"OK," I said, stepping off. I waved as the doors closed, taking Rosie up to the ninth floor, where she worked as a lace cutter. Then I took a deep breath and followed the line of women through a narrow door onto the factory floor.

When I'd first started working at Triangle, Tony had asked me repeatedly what it was like, probably doing research for his work with the unions. I'd told him how the entire space was crammed with rows of long tables that held hundreds of sewing machines. I'd described how the sewing machine operators sat so close together that our elbows bumped. I'd told him how, on hot days, the heat was stifling, and how on cold ones my fingers froze. I'd explained how there weren't enough toilets, and the few we had stank. I'd told him that the floor was littered with piles of fabric, and the fabric bins beneath the long tables were overflowing. I'd shown him the bits of lint that clung to my dress at the end of each day.

What I couldn't fully describe was the noise. When all the machines were running, the sound was incredible. I'd lose part of my hearing most days and wouldn't recover it until I got home. The racket was relentless.

I made my way down the narrow aisle, past the cutting tables, where young women chattered in Italian and Yiddish, to the cloakroom. Inside, I found a hook for my coat and lunch pail.

Suddenly a shadow filled the doorway, blocking my way out of the room. At first I didn't pay much attention. There were always people coming in and out of the cloakroom at the start of the workday. But then the shadow called my name.

CHAPTER FOUR

I jumped, but when I turned, I recognized the
boy standing there watching me. "Oh, Michael,"
I said, pressing my hand to my racing heart. "You
scared me."

"I didn't mean to frighten you, Lucia," Michael
replied in Italian. He took a step toward me. His
eyes darted to mine and then flitted away.

Michael Zerilli was a year older than I was
and training to be a cutter, just like Cara's fiancé,
Frank. His family had come to America a few years
ago. They'd fled Naples after Mount Vesuvius had

erupted, spewing ash into the air. When the ash had landed, the crops had died. Like me—and almost everyone else at Triangle—Michael was one of millions of immigrants looking for a better life in America because we'd run out of options in our old countries.

"Did you . . . want something?" I asked. I knew Michael liked me. He often teased me at lunchtime and smiled shyly whenever he saw me. Once he'd walked me part of the way home.

Michael blushed and ducked his head. "I was wondering if I could walk you home again today."

"Oh," I said. "I'm spending the afternoon with Rosie."

"I see," Michael said slowly. "Then I guess I should give you this now." He reached for my hand, pressing something into my palm. Then he gave me a bashful smile and disappeared from the room.

The smile did something strange to my heart. For a second I felt all wobbly and lightheaded. It was as if I wanted to dance and throw up at the same time.

I took a breath to calm myself and unfolded my hand. I couldn't believe it. Michael had given me a necklace of stars.

I had told Michael about my dream to become an astronomer the day he'd walked me home. Somehow we'd started talking about Halley's Comet, and I'd mentioned how much I liked the stars. At first, he'd thought I meant I just liked to look at them. I'd almost let him believe it. But instead, I'd taken a deep breath and explained that I wanted to study them someday. He was the only person besides Rosie who knew about my dream.

Michael hadn't said much after that, and I'd wondered if he thought I was odd. Maybe he felt the same way my father did, that girls didn't need to go to school.

But now he had given me a necklace of stars.

It was a simple chain with a pendant shaped like a cluster of stars. The necklace was cheap, but it had probably taken Michael months to save up for it. He'd probably started saving the day he walked me home, I realized. I wasn't sure how I felt about that. I liked Michael. Sometimes he made my heart flutter, but I didn't want a boyfriend. A boyfriend only complicated matters.

I made my way down the long aisle to my workstation, dodging the patterns hanging from the ceiling. I elbowed my way to my machine, tripping over the rungs of chairs and bumping my hip on the table. When I finally sat down, I glanced around. Michael watched me from across the crowded factory floor. I gave him a half smile, and he blushed.

Suddenly someone jostled my chair hard from behind. The necklace fell into my lap, and I looked up to see Marcella Rossi looming over me, an angry glint in her hard eyes. Her red hair floated in a cloud around her head.

If I had an enemy at the factory, it was Marcella. She hadn't liked me from the moment I started at Triangle. I think she was jealous of the attention Michael paid me.

At lunch on my very first day, Michael had come over to talk to me. Over his shoulder I had seen Marcella glaring at me. The two of them had come to America from the same village, and I'd seen the way her eyes followed him. But Michael treated Marcella more like a sister than anything.

"Good morning, Marcella," I said politely.

"Where did you get that?" she demanded, motioning to the necklace in my hand.

I closed my hand around the necklace and shoved it deep in my pocket. "It was a gift."

Marcella's face grew pale. "From Michael?"

The words hung over me. I gave a slow nod.

Without another word, Marcella whirled around and stomped back to her table. She made sure to ram the back of my chair on her way past.

I rolled my eyes. I suspected I would be getting jarred a few more times by Marcella before the end of the day.

At that moment, the foreman turned on the electricity. All around me, the sewing machines rumbled to life. The day had begun.

When Cara had first gotten me the job at Triangle, she'd lied and said I knew how to sew. The truth was, I'd never been good with a needle and thread. Mama had tried to teach me to mend clothes a thousand times, but I'd never managed more than a simple stitch. On my first day, I had no idea how to use the sewing machine. The girl to my left had ignored me, but the girl to my right had been Rosie.

"Do you know what you're doing?" she'd asked after watching me fiddle with the machine.

For an instant, I had feared she would turn me in. But then I saw the humorous gleam in her eyes, and I knew I had found a friend.

After Rosie taught me to sew a passable seam, we'd played games to get through the workday. The noise of hundreds of sewing machines made it impossible to talk, so Rosie would give me complex riddles to ponder. I had learned about Fibonacci numbers from a book I'd borrowed from the library.

I knew Rosie loved learning as much as I did, so I'd taught her about the numbers, and sometimes we would calculate the sequence as far as we could in our heads. We would share our answers at the end of the day. We had gotten into the millions before Rosie got promoted and moved to the ninth floor.

Lunch came and went. Michael tried to make his way toward me, but I wasn't ready to talk to him yet. I needed to talk to Rosie about everything first. Instead, I latched onto a group of girls, pretending to listen as they shared factory gossip. Marcella glared at me a few times, but her expression turned smug when Michael stopped to chat with her.

By the end of the day, my body was aching. My back hurt and my neck was stiff. I stretched my cramped fingers and rolled my shoulders. When I'd first started at Triangle, I'd been so sore at the end of the day that I could barely walk home. I was used to it now, but the work was still painful.

Fortunately, we only had to work until four thirty on Saturdays, and it was almost quitting time. My spirits lifted. I would see Rosie soon. Since today was payday, I might even spend a few cents on a new pencil. Maybe I could see if I could pick up Cara's pay too.

My heart froze.

Oh no. Cara. Frank.

I hadn't taken Cara's note to Frank. I had been so distracted by Michael and the necklace that I had totally forgotten to find Frank at lunch.

I drummed my fingers on my workstation. The end of the day was always chaotic, with several hundred people trying to leave the building at once. I noticed some women were already heading to the cloakroom. If I didn't go now, the crowd would make it almost impossible to get to Frank on the ninth floor until everyone else left. I might as well go now. Besides, that way I could find Rosie sooner.

I finished the seam on my last shirtwaist and slipped out of my chair. Everyone was so focused on finishing that no one noticed. Even Marcella didn't try to trip me. I breathed a sigh of relief when I got to the cloakroom. The whole evening spread before me.

I was putting on my coat when something caught my attention.

I was used to the normal end-of-day noises. Women talking about plans and men calling greetings to each other. The sound of tired feet making their way to the elevators. Lunch pails banging against the railing of the stairs.

But today, the sound was different. Something was wrong. I heard a muffled curse. Then I heard someone barking orders. There was a shriek. And then I heard someone shout a single, terrifying word.

"Fire!"

CHAPTER FIVE

I raced to the door of the cloakroom and stared in horror. On the opposite end of the floor, flames sprouted from a bin of fabric scraps.

"Get a bucket!" someone shouted.

The words spurred me into action. I grabbed one of the buckets of water that lined the wall for situations like this. A few of the cutters had already grabbed buckets nearer the flames. I ran as fast as I could to the bin, careful not to slosh any precious liquid over the sides.

"We need more water!" another voice yelled.

A knot of workers crowded around the bin.
I couldn't get through.

"Here," I said, shoving my elbow into someone's
back. He turned and saw what I was holding. I
pushed the bucket into his hands. Then I turned
around to look for more water. My heart sank when
I realized all the buckets had already been used.

"The hose!" I shouted, remembering the fire
hoses on each landing.

My words were swallowed up in the rising panic. People were shouting, and screams pierced the air.

I forced myself to take a deep breath. *Someone will get the fire hose and take care of it,* I told myself. *There will be water, and they'll get the fire out, and we'll all get home safely.*

Then: "No pressure! There's no water pressure!"

As the crowd shifted, I could see a limp fire hose dangling from a man's hand. He shook the hose near

the fire as if hoping water would magically flow out
of the end.

"Get these people out of here!" someone
shouted, although there was no need to say it.
Everyone in the factory had already begun to flee.
People were overturning chairs and shoving each
other out of the way in their panic.

By now, the fire had consumed every bit
of fabric in the scrap bin and was searching for
something new to devour. It found it in the patterns
and cloth that hung from the ceiling. There was a
roar as the fire grew, unfurling itself like a dragon in
a fairy tale. As I gazed at it in horror, I knew that it
wanted to destroy us all.

Workers crowded the Greene Street exit,
pressing against the thin partition that separated the
elevator from the factory floor. I glanced over my
shoulder. On the opposite end of the floor, more
workers crowded the Washington Place doors.

My feet moved before my brain caught up, carrying me away from the heat of the fire and toward the Washington Place doors. Someone stepped on my toes, and I was suddenly knocked against the door of the cloakroom. Panic clawed at my throat. I had just come from the cloakroom! I had made no progress toward safety.

Just then I heard a terrible shout. "It's locked! The doors are locked!"

Frantic screams filled the air.

Of course they're locked, I thought desperately.

The foremen locked us in each day so we wouldn't leave early and so they could search our bags for any stolen scraps of fabric before we left for the day. And now we were locked in with the flames.

Over the din, I could hear a woman yelling frantically, "Fire! I said there's a fire! Tell them! Tell—" Her voice broke off with an anguished cry.

I glanced over and recognized one of the bookkeepers. She clutched the phone to her ear. Her eyes met mine, and she dropped the phone and grasped my arm, her fingers digging into my muscle.

"They don't know," she cried. "They don't know!"

"Who doesn't know?" I asked. I grabbed her elbow to steady her. Her grip was so tight it hurt. "Who doesn't know?"

"The ninth floor," she said. Her eyes were wild. "They don't know about the fire. I called the switchboard, but the operator left to warn the owners before I told her to call the ninth."

"Then call nine!" I yelled, wanting to shake some sense into this woman. Didn't she know that Rosie was on the ninth floor?

"I can't! The phone only connects me to the switchboard on ten!" The woman dissolved into tears. Her hands released me.

Over her shoulder, I saw a foreman wading into the mass of bodies shoving against the Washington Place doors. He was waving keys over his head and shouting something. I saw the crowd part, and the man was instantly swallowed up.

I had no idea if he would make it to the door. But he was our only hope.

"Run!" I pushed the woman toward the doors.

I moved to follow her when a wave of people separated us. I fell against the wall, clutching my throat. The smoke was starting to burn my lungs. My eyes teared up. The crowds around the Washington Place doors hadn't moved. Maybe the foreman hadn't made it. Maybe he had dropped the keys.

Maybe we wouldn't make it out of here.

At that moment, the Green Street elevator doors slid open. *Thank god,* I thought. *People will get on the elevators and get to safety. I'll get there too. We'll all be fine.*

But just then, a gust of wind shuddered through the elevator shaft. It should have been a welcome sign. A breath of spring at the end of a long winter. Instead, it was a gust of doom. The wind stirred the flames, and the fire jumped.

Flames flowed like a river, sliding over mounds of fabric scraps. Eddies of flames licked at the hems of girls' dresses. Puffs of fire floated through the air on clouds of fabric bits, dropping like snow to ignite piles of unfinished shirtwaists.

It was almost beautiful. The flames were mesmerizing in the way they moved and darted. A part of me wanted to study it, to see what it did next.

Then I heard a strange sound coming from inside the cloakroom. I peeked inside, stunned to see a half dozen women huddled together. They were laughing.

"Why are you laughing?" I demanded. "This isn't funny!"

"Miriam!" a stout woman shouted, pushing past me and into the room. "Come with me, sister!"

She managed to grab the arm of one of the giggling women. Other hands tried to pull Miriam back to the ground, but her sister was stronger.

"Get out!" she yelled as she dragged her sister to the door. She repeated the command in Yiddish. It only made the women laugh harder.

"They're in shock," the stout woman said to me. "There is no helping them if they cannot help themselves." She brushed past me, pulling her sister in her wake.

I looked in horror at the women crowded on the floor of the cloakroom. "Go! Get out of here! Save yourselves!" I yelled. I repeated it in both English and Italian.

A few of the women staggered to their feet, dragging others with them out the door. One woman remained hunched in the corner.

"You have to get out of here!" I shouted. "There's still time!"

Her dark eyes met mine. Then she slowly shook her head.

There was a huge crash behind me. I spun around. A wall of fire now blocked the last few rows of tables. Through the flames, I could see girls jumping onto the tabletops. One girl tried to leap to the top of the next table. I recognized her. She sat two machines down from me. My heart dropped as her foot slipped and she fell. The smoke was too thick for me to see if she got up.

I have to get to her, I thought. There was a break in the fire. If I could only get to her aisle, I could reach her and pull her to safety.

I started running, but someone rammed into me. In an instant, I lost my balance, and then I was falling too.

CHAPTER SIX

A strong arm caught me around my waist. I turned and found myself gazing into Michael's soot-smudged face.

"I didn't mean to knock into you," he said, releasing me.

I immediately missed the pressure of his arm. "I know."

Michael's gaze flickered over my shoulder, taking in the terrifying fire. "We need to get out of here."

"I know that too," I said. For the first time since the fire began, I felt a moment of hope. I squeezed

Michael's hand, and he smiled at me. If we had been anywhere else, I might have kissed him.

Behind us, I sensed a sudden release. We looked to see the crowds moving through the now-open Washington Place doors. The foreman must have made his way to the lock.

"Let's go!" Michael said. He clutched my hand, and we started to run toward the doors.

But at that moment, we heard a terrible, familiar scream. Michael drew up short, and I collided with him. I was close enough to hear him whisper a name under his breath: "Marcella."

I followed his gaze, freezing in horror when I realized what I was seeing through the smoke. Marcella, the girl who loved to torment me, was stranded in a sea of fire. She was still at her workstation, frozen in place as the flames crept closer.

"Help me!" she shouted.

"I can't leave her," Michael said, already moving away from me.

I looked back at the open doors for a brief moment, then followed Michael into the flames. Marcella might not be my friend, but no one deserved to die like that.

The heat intensified as Michael and I drew closer to the fire. The flames looked like an angry knot of snakes, hissing and spitting. Michael yelled something in Italian—I didn't quite catch what— and shook his fist at the fire. As if understanding him, the flames shifted and created a gap toward Marcella's workstation.

Michael looked back at me for an instant. "Go!" he said, pointing at the doors. "I'll meet you on the street!" Then he dove neatly into the opening. The wall of fire closed behind him.

"Michael!" I screamed. But he was already gone.

I searched frantically for another opening. I had to get to him. I had to help him with Marcella. Then we would all get to safety.

There was another brief gust of wind from the elevator shaft and everything went hazy. Smoke scorched my lungs and burned my eyes.

"Michael!" I screamed again. "Marcella!"

No one answered my shouts. No one could even hear them. Every noise was swallowed up by the roar of the fire as it slid down the rows of tables, consuming everything in its path.

It was growing so dark from the billowing smoke that I could no longer see anything. It was like being trapped in a nightmare. All that existed was the snap of the fire and the scorching heat. Panic seized my lungs as I ran blindly, trying to get as far from the flames as possible.

If I can just get to the doors, I'll be safe, I thought.

Just then, for a brief moment, the smoke cleared, and I realized I had gotten completely turned around. I was nowhere near the Washington Place stairs.

"This way!" a woman shouted, emerging from the darkness. She pulled a train of four other girls with her.

I grabbed the last girl's skirt. She turned to me, her face wild with terror. "Let go!" she shrieked, trying to kick me loose.

"I'm just trying to get to the door!" I shouted.

The girl kicked again, and I was knocked backward. As I found my feet, stubbornness welled up inside me. Images of my family floated through my head. Papa. Mama. Tony. Alessandra. All the little ones.

I was not going to die here. I was not going to leave them. Not if I could help it.

I launched myself in the direction of the Greene Street doors. At least I hoped it was the right direction. The smoke made it impossible to see, but I knew that I had to get to the doors.

Once I got to the street, I would find Michael and Marcella. I would even hug Marcella and tell her how glad I was that Michael had gone back for her. We would share our stories of how we escaped the blaze. Then we would go home and sleep in our own beds.

I refused to let it be any other way.

I rammed into a crowd of people trying to shove past the thin partition that led to the Greene Street stairs. I looked behind me, hoping to catch a glimpse of Michael or Marcella, but there was only the fire. In the distance, I could hear shrieks and screams. The sounds would haunt me forever.

Holding my breath, I surrendered to the crowd and let myself be swept through the doorway. I was halfway through when my coat caught on the frame. I tugged, but my sleeve was stuck.

"Help!" I yelled. I was trapped in the doorway. Bodies surged around me. The breath was being slowly pressed out of my lungs.

I felt fingers clutch my arm, and I stared into the eyes of a woman who looked to be my mother's age. She shouted something, but I couldn't make out what she was trying to say, and try as I might, I couldn't get free. I was trapped on either side of the doorframe. Heavy shoes crushed my feet. An elbow rammed my abdomen. No one meant to hurt me, but everyone was desperate to get out of the building. And I was stuck here.

The woman who had been shouting at me disappeared. Then I felt a giant tug from behind. The fabric of my coat stretched taut and then tore. I was free.

"Go!" a voice shouted in my ear. I glanced back and saw the woman who had been shouting at me. Her face was streaked with soot. She had fought her way back through the doorway to save me. I clutched her hands, even as she was turning away. For an instant, she cradled my hands in hers.

"Go," she repeated. Then she pushed me to the elevators. I looked back to see her guiding other workers through the partition.

It was even more chaotic on this side of the wall. I could hear shouts as the elevator doors swung open. I could hardly believe the elevators were still running. I didn't want to think about how long they could keep going.

There were more shouts and surges as a mass of humanity pushed its way onto the elevator. "That's all we can take!" I heard the elevator operator shout. "We'll be back for more! I promise!"

The doors closed, and the elevator descended.

People screamed as the flames crept closer. The partition walls were so hot they were glowing. Soon the flames would erupt through the walls.

It was then that I noticed a steady trickle of people racing through the narrow doorway leading to the stairs. The stairs were barely wide enough for one person, but they led outside. And I was determined to get to them.

Tripping and stumbling, I made my way to the landing. The air was slightly cooler here. All I had to do was follow the press of people down the stairs. Then I would be outside. I would be safe.

But then I thought about Michael going after Marcella. I thought about the woman who had freed me from the doorway. I thought about Rosie, and I remembered the bookkeeper saying that the ninth floor hadn't been warned.

I glanced overhead. What if my best friend was trapped? What if she needed me?

Taking a deep breath, I made my choice.

CHAPTER **SEVEN**

Triangle Shirtwaist Factory, ninth floor
March 25, 1911
4:36 p.m.

I raced up the stairs, my feet pounding on the steps. It was hot in the stairwell and strangely empty after the crushing panic of the crowds on the eighth floor. I reached the landing to the ninth floor. Only then did I realize why I hadn't met anyone else coming down the stairs.

The ninth floor was an inferno. The flames roared in my face. They were like a hungry beast attacking everything in sight. Behind the flames, I could see dark shapes twisting and turning. I couldn't tell if I was seeing people or simply more flames. The heat was so intense I could barely open my eyes.

It's odd, I thought, *that the world would end in such brightness. Maybe this is what the comet's tail is like.*

I doubled over coughing, smoke searing my lungs. The air was slightly cooler when I bent down, but a gust of wind brought the flames even closer. Smoke swirled around my legs.

"Rosie!" I shouted, standing upright again. "Rosie!"

There was no way I could even step foot onto the ninth floor. The fire had blocked all the doors. I thought about Frank. Was he up here? I shouted his name too, but no one answered.

"Rosie!" I yelled once more.

Then, impossibly, there she was. The flames drew back for a second, and I saw my best friend. She stood in the middle of a group of women, shouting orders. I could hear snippets of words: "Run . . . fire escape . . . no time."

There were screams behind her. When she turned, I swore she saw me. Even in the middle of the chaos, Rosie smiled at me. Her lips moved, but I couldn't tell what she was saying.

"Rosie!" I shouted. "Be careful! I'll see you outside!"

The curtain of flames fell, and the fire jumped closer to me. I stepped back. There was nothing I could do.

Just then I was jostled from behind. I turned to find a half dozen women crowding up the stairs behind me.

"We're going to die here!" one of them shouted.

"Keep your head down, and get to the fire escape!" someone else commanded. I recognized her as the woman who had saved me from the door.

"You can't get to the fire escape from here," I yelled. "The doors are cut off."

The women stopped on the landing behind me. One of them let out a loud gasp of anguish. "We're trapped."

"No, we're not. Go back down," I said. "We can take the stairs."

The woman from the door looked at me, her gaze level. "The stairs are cut off."

I looked over her shoulder, fear clawing my stomach as I saw tongues of fire licking their way up the stairs. From the ninth floor, the fire pressed closer to the landing, edging us into its fatal grasp.

"The roof!" I yelled, pointing up the stairs. "We need to go up!"

The woman nodded. "This way!" she called, running up the stairs.

The rest of the group raced after her. My back was pressed against the wall. I could feel it growing hotter and hotter.

"We're going to die!" one frantic woman said, gripping my shirt as she went by.

"We are not going to die here, do you understand?" I shouted. I took the woman's elbow and shoved her up the stairs in front of me.

All I have to do is get to the roof, I told myself. *I'll be safe there. Rosie is still alive, and we'll be reunited. It's all going to be OK.*

At that moment, I heard a terrible noise. Over the roar of the fire came the sound of shrieking metal, followed by desperate screams. It sounded as if it was coming from outside the factory.

A devastating realization bloomed inside of me. The fire escape. It had always looked flimsy, barely wide enough for one person. Rosie and I used to joke that in an emergency, it could save one or maybe two people at most. But those were just jokes. The fire escape couldn't have collapsed, could it?

My head tilted as a wave of dizziness swept over me. My knees buckled. "Rosie," I whispered.

I didn't want to move. It was warm and dark in the stairs. The fire was only seconds away, but I no longer saw the use in fighting it. Faces floated through my mind: Rosie, Frank, Michael. Even Marcella. Were any of them still alive? Did I want to live in a world where they were gone?

Suddenly light flashed before my eyes, and a memory jolted me to my feet. I remembered the first time I'd seen Halley's Comet. I'd been standing on a rooftop, my eyes scanning the horizon. I'd spotted the smudge of light and my life had changed. I knew I'd wanted something more. I wasn't going to let the fire take that away.

I got to my feet. I was going to get out of here.

Then my ankle twisted, knocking me against the wall. My head hit the railing and I fell into darkness.

CHAPTER EIGHT

Triangle Shirtwaist Factory, ninth floor
March 25, 1911
4:38 p.m.

Rosie stood over me, her hair haloed by the sun.
She grinned and reached out her hands for mine.
"We'll be late for class," she said.

"Let's stay here a little while longer," I replied.
"It is so nice here."

A bee buzzed past my nose, and I rolled onto
my side to watch it bump into a purple flower. I
stretched and smiled. I had never felt so happy or
at peace.

"Lucy, you'll be late for class," Rosie said again,
her face turning into a frown.

"I don't care," I said. "Let's stay here all day. Let's stay here forever." I never wanted to leave this sweetly scented meadow.

Then the sunlight dimmed, choked by plumes of smoke. Rosie's hands found mine. She tried to tug me to my feet, but I wouldn't move.

"Lucy. Lucy, you have to move," she insisted.

"No, I don't want to," I protested.

"Lucy. Listen to me. You need to move. You need to get out of here."

"But it's nice here," I complained. "I don't want to go."

"Lucy!"

I looked up and saw a monster made of fire wrap its arms around Rosie's waist and snatch her away. I screamed and reached for her, but she had already vanished. Then the monster reached for me.

At that moment, I woke up. I was still in the factory, and the flames were marching closer.

Smoke swirled over my head, reaching down to kiss my face and steal my breath away.

No. I am not going to die here.

I forced myself to my feet, and my ankle immediately buckled underneath me. Pain shot up my leg. I gasped and clung to the railing.

Go, Lucy. Move. Get up the stairs.

The words were a breath. I could barely hear them over the buzzing in my head and the roar of the fire. But I could have sworn it was Rosie's voice in my ear.

I gripped the railing harder and pulled myself up. Smoke threatened to suffocate me, and I fell back to my knees. I gave up on standing. It was easier to crawl up the stairs anyway.

For a long time, all that existed were the rough stairs, the wood hot beneath my palms. My skirt rasped over the steps, and smoke teased my lungs. Pain shot up my leg, and tears streamed down my face.

Finally I reached a step that was slightly wider than the rest. I had reached the tenth-floor landing.

I had never been on the tenth floor before. It belonged to the shipping department, the salesmen, and the factory owners. Soon it would belong to the flames. I remembered that the tenth floor had been warned well in advance. From the stairwell I could see evidence of a hasty evacuation. Several chairs had been overturned, and the skylight had been broken.

I drew a deep breath and kept crawling up the stairs to the roof. The air was cooler now, and there was less smoke. Midway up, I saw a shadow.

"Rosie?" I whispered, my voice filled with desperate hope.

"There you are!" an unfamiliar voice replied. Footsteps pounded on the stairs, and I was lifted to my feet.

"Ankle," I gasped.

"Lean against me," the voice said as a strong arm encircled me. It was the woman who had saved me from the door. "We'd wondered where you'd gone. They're trying to get us off the roof as quickly as possible, but I said I was going back for you."

"They?" I rasped.

"The law students from next door," the woman explained. "They lowered a ladder from the top of their building to ours. They're getting people to safety."

"People? There are more of us who got to the roof?" I asked.

The woman nodded as she helped me up the final step. "You'll see. A bunch of us got to the roof, including the owners. They bolted right away. Figures," she grumbled under her breath.

Her words left me with hope, even in the middle of this terrible day. Maybe Rosie had made it to the roof after all.

My savior kept her arm around me as she led me across the rooftop. Smoke was coming up the sides of the building now and billowing through the broken skylight. It was getting difficult to see. I could hear people screaming from below.

The initial excitement I'd felt faded quickly. We might be out of the building, but we were still in the grip of the fire.

"Keep going," the woman said. She led me across the roof and toward a ladder. From the roof next door, several well-dressed students were helping frightened people climb to safety.

"Wait," I said, stopping so quickly the woman stumbled against me. My ankle throbbed with pain. "My friend. Rosie. I have to see if she's here."

The woman shook her head. "Listen to me. We need to get you to safety. You can look for your friend on the roof of the law school."

"She was on the ninth floor," I whispered.

The woman's face grew serious. "Then you can look for her on the roof next door. If she got to safety, she'll be there."

If? I thought.

"The fire escape!" I shouted. "She was trying to get to the fire escape. Maybe she came up to the roof!"

I broke free of the woman's grasp and hobbled toward the wall that overlooked the inner courtyard. I could hear shouting behind me. A part of me knew I was being irrational. I didn't even remember if the fire escape came up to the roof. But if Rosie was here, I would find her.

"Stop! Stop her!"

I elbowed my way past a half dozen confused factory workers. I peered frantically into each of their faces. I saw shock and confusion, loss and pain reflected back at me. But none of them was Rosie.

Behind me, the woman was still shouting. But I wouldn't stop. I had to get to Rosie.

I reached the corner of the building. I had gotten turned around in the smoke and couldn't tell if I was near the fire escape or not. But I leaned over the side of the building and shouted anyway.

"Rosie! Rosie!"

At that moment, flames shot over the side of the building.

"Stop it!" I screamed. The fire twisted and taunted me. "Stop! I won't let you win!"

The flames dipped and darted, reaching for me. I was too slow. In an instant, my skirt caught on fire.

CHAPTER **NINE**

Triangle Shirtwaist Factory roof
March 25, 1911
4:44 p.m.

Last summer, on my fourteenth birthday, my
family had picnicked in Washington Square Park.
It was one of the few times that everyone in my
family had been happy. My father and Tony hadn't
argued. The little ones had run and played on the
green. Even my mother had smiled from time to
time.

At the end of the afternoon, we'd discovered
that a line of ants had somehow found our food
scraps. They were marching up the side of the
picnic basket.

I had been fascinated by how single-minded and orderly they were. They'd been determined to reach the food, and nothing was going to stop them.

That's what the flames looked like on my skirt. An army of flame ants marching steadily up my leg. The sight was mesmerizing.

A part of my brain screamed at me to move and extinguish the fire. But I couldn't stop staring. The fire had already consumed so much. Now it was trying to consume me.

"Get her down!" someone shouted. Hands landed on my shoulders and pressed me to the rooftop. Other hands twisted the worn fabric of my skirt until the flames had been suffocated.

"That was close," a male voice said.

I looked up into the soot-streaked face of a handsome young man. I assumed he was one of the law students. He had extinguished the flames, and his hand was still tangled in my skirt.

I stifled a giggle. Then I hiccupped and started to sob.

Someone helped me to my feet. It was the woman who had been with me since the eighth floor.

"You keep saving me," I said.

Her arm tightened around my shoulder for a second. "Let's go," she said.

"You know the way to the ladder?" the man asked. His face was pale underneath his tan, but his voice was sure.

"Yes," the woman said.

"Good. Now go. I need to see if anyone else is still on this roof." He disappeared into the smoke, and the woman and I hobbled our way to the ladders.

"Whatever you do, don't look down," she whispered.

I nodded to show that I had heard. Then I climbed my way to safety.

I don't remember how long I sat on the roof of
the law school. There were several groups of us up
there, huddled together in shock. We watched as
smoke continued to billow and flames licked the
sides of the Asch Building. At one point, someone
dropped a shawl over my shoulder and helped me
to the stairs.

I looked for the woman who had helped me,
but she had disappeared. I hadn't even learned her
name.

When I got to the street, I clutched the shawl
closer around my shoulders and began searching the
face of every survivor.

I didn't find Rosie.

"Lucia!" someone called. The voice was half
hope, half sob.

I turned as quickly as my ankle would allow. "Marcella," I whispered, hobbling over to where she hunched on the sidewalk.

She reached for me, wrapping her arms around me. For a long time, I held her as she cried. Deep, heaving sobs tore through her body. I smoothed her hair and murmured in Italian.

Finally, Marcella drew back. Her eyes were red, and her face streaked with char. "It was horrible," she started. "It happened so quickly. One moment I was getting ready to leave. The next moment I was trapped by the fire. And Michael—"

Her voice broke on his name, and in that moment, I knew. Michael had not survived.

"He saved me," Marcella said. "He got me out."

"And then what?" My voice was a whisper.

"He went back. There were others. Other girls who had machines nearer the window. Nearer the wall. It could have been any of us," she said.

I nodded. She was right. It could have been any of us.

"He went back to try to save them," Marcella said again. "That was the last I saw."

"Maybe . . . maybe he got out?" I said desperately. I hated to raise our hopes, but if she hadn't seen Michael die, maybe he was still alive. Maybe he got out. Maybe he was on the other side of the block. Maybe he was looking for us.

Marcella shook her head. "He . . . they were trapped. I heard from others."

Her voice trailed off, and I felt my heart sink into my stomach. "There was no way out," I said.

"No way out," Marcella repeated.

I sat with her for a long time after that, neither of us saying anything. At some point Marcella's family appeared, surrounding her with tears and hugs. I didn't know any of them, but they hugged me too.

Eventually they began to lead her home. As she started to walk away, I dug in my pocket.

"Marcella!"

She turned, and I shoved something into her hand. "Here," I said. "You should have this."

Marcella's face crumpled when she opened her palm. The little star pendant winked up at her. "You are sure?" she asked.

I nodded.

Tears filled her eyes. "I should give it back to you," she said. "I shouldn't be so selfish but . . ."

"It's yours," I repeated.

Marcella smiled weakly. "Thank you, Lucia. And . . . I'm so sorry. About your friend Rosie."

The blood chilled in my veins. "What about Rosie?"

Marcella's face grew pale. "Oh no," she said. "I thought you knew. I thought you had already heard when you found me."

My world froze for a moment. If I didn't ask the question and didn't hear the answer, there was still a chance Rosie was alive. But I could not hold off the weight of the universe.

"What happened?" I asked. I barely recognized my own voice.

Marcella laid her hand on my shoulder. "She was on the fire escape. I heard from someone who saw. It was too narrow, too weak. There were too many people on it."

"What happened?" I repeated, my voice hollow. But even as I asked, I knew. I remembered the sound of shrieking metal.

"It collapsed. It tore away from the building and collapsed. They all fell."

Marcella's family led her away, and I sank to the sidewalk, hollow with grief.

CHAPTER **TEN**

Bleecker Street, New York City
March 25, 1911
8:00 p.m.

In the end, there was nothing left to do but go home. Worried faces streamed toward me as I made my way up Bleecker Street. I could feel eyes on me, hoping I was the daughter or sister or friend they were looking for. I realized it was possible my family didn't even know about the fire yet. Tony would still be at work, and Papa rarely left the house.

I tucked my hands into my pockets as I limped home. I had lost my hat somewhere in the flames, but I was still wearing my coat. My fingertips brushed paper—Cara's note to Frank.

I stopped short. I had never given it to him. I couldn't believe I had forgotten about my cousin and her fiancé so quickly. I hadn't seen Frank in the crowds of survivors, but maybe . . .

I shoved the note deeper into my pocket and continued home.

The sidewalk in front of my building was crowded when I limped up. I could hear frantic voices.

"If she's there, we have to go."

"Someone has to stay here in case she comes home!" my father shouted.

I realized they were talking about me. I opened my mouth. My voice was hoarse from the smoke.

"Here," I whispered. "I'm here."

They didn't hear me. I took another step closer to them. All of the strength I'd used to get here drained away. I swayed on the sidewalk, watching my family argue about what they should do next. I saw anger, grief, and despair in their faces.

Then I saw my mother's face, drawn and pale in the fading light.

"Mama," I whispered.

Somehow she heard me. Her face turned toward me. All of the others stopped talking and followed the direction of her gaze.

"Lucy," Mama whispered. She stepped out of the group of people, followed by Tony and my father. Her arms were outstretched, and I fell into them.

New York City
March 26–28, 1911

The next few days were a blur. Reports about the fire spread quickly through the neighborhood. We learned that the firemen had responded immediately, but their ladders had only reached the sixth floor. Their equipment had not caught up with the size of the new factory buildings. The firemen had bravely gone up the stairs and put out the blaze before it had burned down the entire building. We heard about the heroism of the elevator operators, who'd made several runs and saved dozens of lives. We heard story after story of those who'd survived, dashing down the stairs at the last minute.

And we began to list the names of the dead. In the end, 146 of us died. Some of us, like Michael, had been trapped by the flames. Others, like Rosie, died on the fire escape. And there were others the fire had chased to the windows. They'd jumped, knowing it was unlikely they would survive the fall. We heard about families who had lost two daughters, husbands who had lost their wives, brothers who had lost a sister.

Anger spread—more quickly than the flames themselves had—with the reports of locked doors, cramped aisles, and the broken fire escape. Tony had a dark glint in his eyes. His voice caught every time he mentioned Rosie's name.

"This could have been prevented," he said. "If the union had succeeded. They could have demanded safer working conditions. Think of what might have been different if the owners hadn't broken the strike a few years ago."

I didn't say anything. I knew he was right, and he knew I agreed with him. Even Papa didn't argue.

The hardest interaction was with Cara. She appeared on our doorstep the day after the fire, clinging to the arm of a friend.

"He's dead," she said, collapsing into a chair. We all knew she was talking about Frank. "He's dead, and I'm not."

"Be happy you live," Mama said, pressing Cara's hand. "You live without Frank, but you live."

Cara crumpled into Mama's arms, and Mama rocked her while she sobbed.

Before she left, Cara took my hand. "My only comfort is that he had my note at the end. He knew my thoughts and my heart." Her eyes searched mine. "You gave him the note, yes?"

I covered her hand with mine, not hesitating for an instant. "Yes," I lied. "I gave him the note."

Lower Manhattan, New York City
April 5, 1911

It rained the day of the memorial procession. Thousands of us lined the route that wound through Washington Square Park, standing stoically under black umbrellas. The International Ladies' Garment Workers' Union had organized the procession to honor the dead and call for massive reform. What happened at Triangle should never happen again.

I held Mama's arm, and Tony stood at my elbow. His tears ran freely down his face. I knew he was thinking about Rosie. We both were.

I couldn't shake the feeling that it could have
been me. It could have been me on that fire escape.
It could have been Rosie standing here in the rain,
suffocating with grief. Or both of us might have
died. Or lived.

I had survived because I'd gone to the cloakroom early. Because I'd gone *up* the stairs instead of down. Because that heroic woman had come back for me again and again.

But I could have easily turned left instead of right. I could have hesitated a moment too long on the stairs. The fire might have jumped a second sooner and caught my clothes.

I hadn't survived because I was somehow better or luckier than those who'd died. I'd survived because that's just the way it worked out. I would have to live with that knowledge for the rest of my life.

I didn't know what awaited me. I knew I still wanted to go to college. I wanted to fulfill the dreams I'd once shared with Rosie. If nothing else, I wanted to live the life that was mine, whatever it brought.

I couldn't do anything else.

A NOTE FROM THE AUTHOR

When I told one of my friends that I was working
on a novel about the Triangle Shirtwaist Factory fire,
she said, "Oh, I love that fire!" Then she laughed, a
little embarrassed, and said, "Well, it's not something to
love. It was horrific. So many people died. But the fire
is fascinating because all these aspects of American life
came together at a pivotal moment, and the fire ushered
in countless changes."

As I discovered through my research, my friend was
right. The fire at the Triangle Shirtwaist Factory captured
the public's imagination from the beginning. Newspaper
accounts from the time describe the horror of the crowd
gathered on the sidewalks, watching helplessly as girls,
women, and men—left with no other choice—jumped
from the flaming windows. The fire escape, like the one
Rosie fled to in this story, *did* tragically collapse, sending
another two dozen people to their deaths. Other workers
tried to slide down the elevator cables—few survived.

Although the fire department responded to news
of the fire almost immediately, their equipment had

not kept up with the building boom in New York City. The ladders were too short to reach the eighth, ninth, and tenth floors of the Asch Building, where the factory was located. Nor did they have the proper equipment to save those who jumped. Of the nearly five hundred people employed at the factory, 146 workers died, most of them young Italian and Jewish immigrant girls, like Lucy and Rosie.

The death of so many young women, most of whom had come to America in search of better lives, struck a chord with the public. And the fire *was* preventable. Imagine how things might have been different had the doors not been locked, had the aisles not been cluttered, had the stairs been wider, had the factory conducted fire drills.

The factory owners could have made changes after the strike by the International Ladies' Garment Workers' Union in 1910. But the owners, Isaac Harris and Max Blanck, had broken the strike and did not make safety improvements.

Harris and Blanck were actually on the tenth floor the day the fire broke out and escaped by fleeing to

A shirt factory sewing room in the early 1900s. Factories were crowded, dark, and dirty and had few safety regulations to protect workers. Long hours and dangerous conditions were a way of life.

the roof. They were charged with manslaughter but were acquitted on December 27, 1911, as it could not be proved they knew beyond a doubt that the doors had been locked at the time of the fire.

They were, however, found guilty of wrongful death in a civil suit in 1913 and ordered to pay seventy-five dollars per casualty. It bears mentioning, though, that Harris and Blanck's insurance company paid *them* about sixty thousand dollars, or about four hundred dollars per death.

Today, the Asch Building still stands. It was donated to New York University in 1929 and renamed the Brown

Building. It now houses the university's biology and chemistry departments.

Beyond the loss of life, I was most saddened to discover that the conditions at the Triangle Shirtwaist Factory were not unique for the time. After the fire, the state of New York established the Factory Investigating Commission, which was tasked with investigating workplaces and interviewing thousands of workers. The commission discovered that many safety improvements needed to be made.

Those discoveries resulted in changes to building codes and workplace safety measures. Many of the safety standards we take for granted—including sturdy fire escapes and fire drills—stem directly from the response to the Triangle Shirtwaist Factory fire.

While I was writing this novel, the biggest challenge I faced was making sure Lucy witnessed as much of the fire as possible. While Lucy was compelled to go up the stairs to save her friend, the workers who had the best chances of survival were those on the eighth floor. Many were able to escape down the Greene Street stairs. Almost none of the workers on the ninth floor survived.

The fire escape at Triangle Shirtwaist Factory collapsed during the deadly fire on March 25, 1911. It was the only fire escape at the factory and was so narrow it would have taken hours for all the workers to escape using it, even if it hadn't collapsed.

Much of Lucy's experience of the fire was informed by oral history interviews of survivors, which you can hear by visiting the Triangle Fire Online Exhibit from Cornell University. As a writer and a librarian, I can't emphasize enough how valuable these interviews are. Not only do they give us insight into the fire itself, they also give us a better understanding of the lives these women and men led.

My research did have some bright spots. I loved learning about the vibrant immigrant neighborhoods that made up New York City's Greenwich Village, although I reminded myself not to romanticize Lucy's life. Her life was difficult. As a young woman in 1910, she had few options, and college was a nearly unreachable goal.

Families like Lucy's were often hovering on the edge of poverty, facing almost impossible odds in their struggle to create a better life with more financial security. Their rent could have fluctuated monthly with little warning from landlords. Sometimes families were charged extra rent if they had more children!

I can't imagine the stress of finding extra money at a moment's notice or being evicted from your home. I was also struck by how immigrant families and communities today still face tremendous challenges. I hope Lucy's story helps us all build compassion for our fellow human beings.

While the factory fire forms the core of this story, Lucy is unaware of that fact until the end of Chapter Four. I wanted to make sure readers had a sense of Lucy's life, including her hopes, dreams, and fears, independent of the fire itself. She is a young woman unhappy with the many restrictions that mark her life, but she also keeps dreaming of a life that is her own. My final hope is that Lucy's commitment inspires all of us to continue pursuing our deepest dreams.

GLOSSARY

eddies (ED-eez)—currents of air or water running against a main current or in a circle

Fibonacci numbers (fee-boh-NAH-chee NUHM-berz)—an unending sequence of numbers in which the first two numbers are 1 and 1, and each number that follows is the sum of the two preceding numbers (1, 1, 2, 3, 5, 8, 13, 21, 34, and so on)

Halley's Comet (HAL-eez KOM-it)—a comet that passed by Earth in 1910, causing a widespread panic that Earth would be destroyed due to the fact that the planet passed through the comet's tail

immigration (im-i-GREY-shuhn)—an act or instance of coming into a foreign country to live

irrational (ir-RASH-uh-nl)—not able to reason

Mount Vesuvius (mount vuh-SOO-vee-uhs)—an active volcano 4,190 feet (1,277 meters) high in the region of Campania, Italy, on the Bay of Naples; its erruption in 1906 killed more than one hundred people.

negotiate (ni-GOH-shee-eyt)—to have a discussion with another in order to settle something

persecutions (pur-si-KYOO-shuhnz)—acts of continual harm or cruelty

pogrom (puh-GRUHM)—the organized killing of many helpless people, usually because of their race or religion

poverty (POV-er-tee)—lack of money or possessions

prestigious (pre-STIJ-uhs)—honored or esteemed

prosperous (PROS-per-uhs)—strong and healthy in growth

shirtwaist (SHURT-weyst)—a woman's tailored garment (such as a blouse or dress) with details copied from men's shirts

tenement (TEN-uh-muhnt)—a building divided into separate apartments for rent

union (YOON-yuhn)—an organization of workers formed to help them get better pay and working conditions

MAKING CONNECTIONS

1. At the end of this story, Lucy reflects on the fact that she survived not because she was lucky or chosen to survive. Instead, she concludes, that's just how things worked out. Do you agree with Lucy's views? Why or why not?

2. Many factors contributed to the tragedy of the Triangle Shirtwaist Factory fire. Identify some of the key reasons why the fire was so deadly. What do you think could have been done differently to prevent the tragedy? Who, if anyone, do you think was ultimately responsible for the fire?

3. After surviving the fire, Lucy decides she needs to live a life that is hers. Imagine Lucy at age eighty, looking back on her life. What do you think her life looked like? Did she go to college and become an astronomer? Did she follow another path? How do you think the fire continued to impact her life?

ABOUT THE AUTHOR

Although Julie Gilbert's masterpiece, *The Adventures of Kitty Bob: Alien Warlord Cat,* has sadly been out of print since she last stapled it together in the fourth grade, Julie continues to write. She is the author of the Dark Waters series from Stone Arch Books. Her novels consider themes of identity and belonging, often with a healthy dose of fantasy and magic. Her short fiction explores topics ranging from airport security lines to adoption to antique wreaths made of hair. She is especially committed to diversity in her writing. Julie makes her home in southern Minnesota with her husband, children, and two lazy cats.